THE DISGUSTING ADVENTURES OF

FLEABAG MONKEYFACE

INVASION of the

GRUBBY SNATCHERS

KNIFE & PACKER

WALKER
BOOKS

The authors would like to dedicate this book
to the inventor of the space toilet, without
whom all astronauts would have to live in
seriously pongy space stations!

First published 2009 by Walker Books Ltd
87 Vauxhall Walk, London SE11 5HJ

2 4 6 8 10 9 7 5 3

© 2009 Duncan McCoshan and Jem Packer

The right of Duncan McCoshan and Jem Packer to be identified
as author/illustrator of this work has been asserted by them
in accordance with the Copyright, Designs and Patents Act 1988

This book has been typeset in Shinn Light

Printed and bound in Great Britain by Clays Ltd, St Ives plc

British Library Cataloguing in Publication Data:
a catalogue record for this book is available
from the British Library

ISBN 978-1-4063-1404-5

www.walker.co.uk

A NOTE FROM THE PUBLISHER

<u>We apologize for what you are about to read!</u>

You may find the images of **spring-cleaning aliens**, **extreme mopping** and **gratuitous showering** disturbing...

We suggest you hide an extra smelly sock behind your wardrobe, *un*make your bed and spill some dirty bath water to make yourself feel better.

Because this story contains scenes of **extreme tidiness**.

So don't tell us we didn't warn you!

But before we get to the horrible clean stuff, let's meet our heroes, **Gerald**, **Gene** and **Fleabag Monkeyface**. Here's a few things you need to know about them:

Gene
Likes: Making lists, especially of gross things
Dislikes: Bunny rabbits
Favourite word: "Unreal"
You should know: Gene has the ideas

Gerald
Likes: The sound of a toilet flushing
Dislikes: Clean towels
Favourite word: "Cool"
You should know: Gerald has the stupid habit of liking Gene's ideas

Fleabag Monkeyface
Likes: Eating nits
Dislikes: Baths, showers and soap
Favourite word: "Ug-brilliant"
You should know: He's got Gross-Out Power

Without Gerald, Gene and Fleabag, the world would be a much cleaner, shinier place.

But let's start at the beginning...

1 Gerald, Gene and Fleabag Monkeyface were hard at work...

"We need more squirrel droppings," said Gene as he squinted at a test tube.

"Yes," said Gerald. "And an extra rotten prawn head."

"And here are those ug-toenail clippings," said Fleabag, holding out a revolting ingredient of his own. "I just ug-love working on school projects!"

Now you may think that squirrel droppings, rotten prawn heads and toenails are pretty gross ingredients for a school project, but Gerald, Gene and Fleabag were always adding a bit of gross-out when they shouldn't...

In fact, Gerald, Gene and Fleabag's love of gross-out was always getting them into trouble!

AAAATCHOO!

UNREAL!

One sports day, **Gerald** sneezed **Dr Cheese's Fungal Foot Powder** all over the gym teacher.

During Book Week, **Gene** read the first six chapters of *The Treatment of Tropical Bottom Boils* out loud, and the entire class had to be sent home sick.

COOL!

UG-BRILLIANT!

SPLAT!

And on International Food Day, **Fleabag Monkeyface** dived face first into the seafood paella.

"I think the **Gross-Out Rocket Fuel** is ready,"
Gene said, wincing as he examined the stinking liquid.
"Fleabag, is the craft in position?"

"Ug-primed and ug-ready to go!" said Fleabag.

"I hope the **Galactic Grossblaster** can survive outer
space," said Gerald. "We did reinforce all the toilet rolls."

Gene carefully poured the bubbling liquid into the
rocket's fuel tank. "Now stand back and get ready for
blast off!" he said.

The mixture fizzled and spluttered. Then, with a loud bang, it ignited – their rocket was airborne!

"We've done it! Now we can explore new galaxies, meet aliens—" said Gene.

But he was interrupted by an even louder...

The rocket juddered and plummeted in a cloud of smoke. The fuel tank had exploded – *again*.

"But we were so close," Gerald said. "Our project will never be ready in time for **School Space Week** now."

"We'll just have to rebuild it," groaned Gene. "Did anyone see where it landed?"

Even though Gerald, Gene and Fleabag spent all afternoon searching for the remains of the Galactic Grossblaster, they just couldn't find them anywhere.

2 School Space Week started the very next day, and a very special guest was coming to visit – **Chip Asteroid**! Chip had travelled the length and breadth of the galaxy filming his hit TV show "Chip Asteroid: Man on a Mission".

"His last TV programme was unbelievable," said Gerald. "He landed his spacecraft single-handed while juggling space helmets!"

"I can't wait to meet a real-life astronaut," said Gene, as they filed into the school hall.

"And we've got ug-permission to ug-film afterwards!" said Fleabag excitedly.

Gerald, Gene and Fleabag had their own TV show, Gross-Out TV – although their disgusting adventures always seemed to get in the way of them actually making any programmes.

Suddenly a man in a spacesuit bounced out from behind the huge curtain that was covering the stage.

"It's Chip Asteroid!" Gerald beamed.

Everyone cheered ... until the spaceman opened his visor. "Hello and hooray for Space Week!" said Mr Troutman, the class teacher. "Pens at the ready because here are ten *really* interesting **Space Facts**." The class groaned.

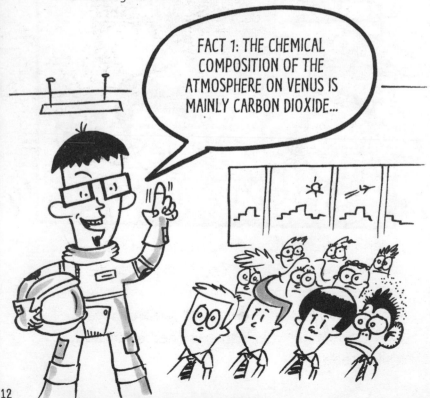

FACT 1: THE CHEMICAL COMPOSITION OF THE ATMOSPHERE ON VENUS IS MAINLY CARBON DIOXIDE...

"When we interview Chip we'll find out some much more *interesting* facts," whispered Gerald.

"There's got to be lots of gross stuff in space," said Gene.

"I can't ug-wait to ug-find out!" said Fleabag, then yawned as Mr Troutman droned on through his Space Facts.

Finally, the curtain was swept back to reveal Space Legend Chip Asteroid hanging out in his **Space Station**!

"When I'm not on a space walk or battling meteor storms, this is where I live. Let me show you around!"

Everyone cheered as Chip finished his guided tour with a display of weightless gymnastics.

"Well, I'm sure we would all like to be astronauts now," gushed Mr Troutman. "Let's give Mr Asteroid a huge round of applause!"

As the rest of the school hurried to lunch, Gerald, Gene and Fleabag stayed behind to meet the great man himself.

"Mr Asteroid has been kind enough to grant you an exclusive interview," said Mr Troutman. "Now, I don't want anything silly or gross to happen."

"Thanks for allowing us to film, Mr Asteroid,"
said Gene after Mr Troutman had left.

"No problem. I was the first man EVER to give
a live TV interview in space." Chip grinned cheesily.

"Fleabag, get ready," said Gerald. "We're going to
ask you a few questions, Mr Asteroid, then we'd like
to film the **Space Toilet**."

"Hit me baby!" Chip grinned again. "I'm ready
to answer!"

Fleabag, microphone at the ready, stepped into position. The camera was rolling – filming had begun!

"So, Mr ug-Asteroid, what happens if you ug-sneeze in ug-space? With no ug-gravity, do all the ug-bits just ug-float around?"

"Sneeze? In space? Do you think a top athlete and fully trained astronaut like me would ever *sneeze* in space?!" said Chip indignantly. "I was the first man EVER to train himself not to sneeze, cough or hiccup in space."

"And what about when you ug-brush your ug-teeth?" probed Fleabag. "When you ug-spit the ug-toothpaste out, does it all ug-fly around?"

"We use edible toothpaste," said Chip. "Did you know I was the first man EVER to floss in space?"

"Is it true that in ug-space, no one can ug-hear you ug-burp?" asked Fleabag.

"What kind of a question is *that*?" said Chip testily.

"OK. That's the interview done," said Gerald, who could see that Chip wasn't in the mood for any more gross-out questions.

"Let's proceed to the Space Toilet," said Gene.

4 "**O**k, guys, here it is," said Chip. "I was the first man EVER to set a Space Toilet to super-suction overdrive, for that really *super*-clean feeling. You see a space toilet is like a giant vacuum cleaner – when you flush, everything gets sucked away. And in super-suction mode, we'd be sucked away too. So no flushing!"

"Ug-fascinating," said Fleabag, who wasn't really listening. "So what does this ug-lever do?"

"**Noooooo!**" screeched Chip. "That's the flush!"

There was a high-pitched sucking noise, then a crack as the handle broke loose.

The Space Toilet was in full-flush mode and no one was safe from its power! First Gerald, then Gene and finally Fleabag were sucked out.

Luckily, the pipe wasn't connected to a sewage tank, so they were all just spat out on the floor of the hall. Chip was less lucky – too big for the pipe, he got wedged in!

"Help! I'm stuck!" he wailed.

"Oh no! It's like **King Pong** all over again!" said Gerald.*

The toilet was still sucking and the whole Space Station was starting to shake and judder. The pressure was too much – it was about to blow!

"Use Gross-Out Power, Fleabag!" said Gene.

PING!
PING!
PING!

Filthy Footnotes
* See The Disgusting Adventures of Fleabag Monkeyface: King Pong

"Time for an ug-turbo sneeze!" cried Fleabag, clambering back on-board the Space Station.

With a huge power surge and a secure grip on Chip, Fleabag let fly, propelling them both into the air.

There was a loud **POP!** as Chip broke loose and flew off the toilet. The flush mechanism coughed, spluttered and finally conked out.

"You saved him!" cried Gerald.

"Great job, Fleabag!" said Gene.

But the space celebrity was looking noticeably disgusted as he dusted himself down.

"That's it. Show's over!" he barked. He couldn't wait to get away – school seemed like a much more dangerous place than any hostile planet. "Nothing like that has EVER happened to me in space."

As soon as Mr Troutman discovered what had happened, he grabbed the film gear. Then he turned on Gerald, Gene and Fleabag.

"Your camera is going in the confiscation cupboard, FOR EVER!" he said. The groaning, messy cupboard was already overflowing with stuff – most of it belonging to Gerald, Gene and Fleabag!

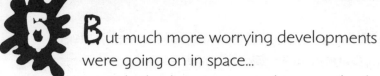

5 **B**ut much more worrying developments were going on in space...

A sleek, gleaming spaceship was silently orbiting Earth. And this was no ordinary spaceship – **Grub Buster 1** was from the faraway planet of **Kleanon**, the shiniest and cleanest planet in the whole universe!

Let's see what was happening on-board...

"They call this filthy blob 'Earth', Skweeky-Kleen," said **Commander Skrubbupp**, addressing his second in command. "It looks so horribly messy. And so does this screen. Polish it immediately!"

"Of course, Oh Uber-Supervisor of Spick and Span," said **Skweeky-Kleen**, pulling out a cloth.

"Planet Earth is inhabited by one of the messiest life forms we have ever come across – 'People' and more specifically **'Children-People'**," continued Skrubbupp.

"*Children-People?*" Skweeky-Kleen shuddered.

"Yes, they are a slovenly, untidy bunch. And they must be stopped!" moaned Skrubbupp. "I feel dirty just thinking about them." He released the Personal Shower Unit attached to his back and doused himself in warm soapy water.

"For years we, the Kleanons, have had a mission," he said. *"A mission that has taken us far from our beautifully shiny home planet of Kleanon, to explore shabby galaxies, to seek out and tidy grotty planets – to boldly clean where no alien has cleaned before!*

"We sanitized the unwashed Lizard-men of Zurbicon 3...

"We deloused the nit-infested Furballs of the Sazmax Galaxy...

"And we banished the planets we could not clean to the back of the universe – to spend eternity on the Intergalactic Naughty Step. **BECAUSE WE ARE THE GRUBBY SNATCHERS!**

"And our triumphant struggle against our arch-nemeses the **Mucrons of Planet Mucroid** is now taught in every school on Kleanon. Let me show you..."

School Textbook

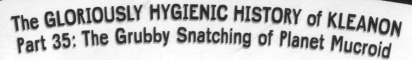

The GLORIOUSLY HYGIENIC HISTORY of KLEANON
Part 35: The Grubby Snatching of Planet Mucroid

For years, the Kleanons had searched for a way to defeat the Mucrons and their home planet of Mucroid. All had failed until the brave and valiant Commander Skrubbupp devised an ingenious ruse to approach the stinking planet – by disguising Grub Buster 1 with rotting seaweed.

Using their protective Anti-Dirt Suits (see Close-Up, opposite), Kleanon forces were able to repel the Mucrons' spaceship-melting bad breath.

The Kleanons dodged toxic slimeballs to capture the Mucrons before they could inflate themselves into giant balls of filth.

Defeated, the Mucrons were snatched, along with their home planet, and put on the Intergalactic Naughty Step. And Queen Mucron's child, Baby Mucron, was taken to be an exhibit in Kleanon Zoo.

Close-Up of the KLEANON ANTI-DIRT SUIT
(design © Commander Mopgood Skrubbupp)

Protective Anti-Dirt Suit: made from high-tech space-age material "Contra-Dust", it ensures no dirt can settle.

Personal Shower Unit: press the release button for an instant warm shower in clean soapy water.

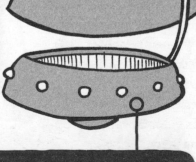

Flotation Pod: float instead of walking. Never touch the dirty ground again!

"But nothing has prepared us for the Children-People of Earth," said Skrubbupp, snapping the book shut.

6 ack on Earth, Gerald, Gene and Fleabag were going to the **Gross-Out Den** (the disused outdoor toilet at the end of Gerald's garden where Fleabag lived). Gerald's mum was waiting for them.

"Hi, guys," she said. "I was just helping Uncle Derrick clear out his loft and I found this. It's an old wooden leg – hollow and full of woodworm. I thought you could use it to make a new rocket."

"Gross!" said Gerald and Gene together.

"Your mum's great," said Gene, entering the Den. "Most parents would make us tidy this place up."

"And this ug-wooden leg is ug-brilliant," said Fleabag. "If we ug-attach the wings here and put the ug-fuel tank ug-here..."

"I think it's a bit too heavy for a rocket," said Gerald. "Maybe you should just put it in the **Gross-Out Museum**."

"I ug-suppose so," said Fleabag, placing it next to a mouldy glass eye and a set of decaying false teeth. "Let's all have an ug-cup of my ug-homemade tea! It's my own ug-blend – 100% dried ug-compost!"

"We need our luck to change," said Gene, who like Gerald had decided *not* to try a cup of Fleabag's tea. "First we lose our rocket, then we have all our film gear and loads of great footage taken away!"

"At least things can't get any worse," said Gerald.

Just then there was a knock at the door...

OH NO! IT'S THE SMUGLEYS!

Randy and Mandy Smugley were the twins who lived next door. They were the complete opposite of Gerald, Gene and Fleabag, and loved soft and cuddly clean things, like mountain springs and fluffy hamsters.

"You lot had better come over sharpish!" bossed Randy, who like his sister was in his smartest clothes. "You've really done it this time!"

"We've got a photographer stuck up a tree in our garden," said Mandy, "*and it's all your fault!!!*"

"What's a photographer doing in *your* garden?" asked Gene.

"It's not any old photographer," said Mandy proudly, "it's showbiz super-snapper Claudio Click!"

"Why would anyone want to take pictures of *you*?" Gerald chuckled.

"It's a photo shoot for *Tidy!* magazine, if you must know," said Randy. "We've won the **World's Tidiest Bedroom Award** for the third year running. Look!"

Suddenly they heard a shout from next door: "Get that thing away from me!"

Gerald, Gene and Fleabag ran outside to see what the noise was.

"The Galactic Grossblaster!" said Gene, spying their lost rocket. "So that's where it ended up!"

Claudio Click had been so disgusted by the rocket, he'd climbed a tree to get away from it.

"Our luck *has* changed," said Gerald. He quickly scooped up the rocket.

Claudio Click finally agreed to come down from the tree ... but only after Gerald, Gene and Fleabag had left.

7 Back on Grub Buster 1, the Kleanons' plot was advancing at a terrifying rate.

"The Kleansulator – our most powerful laser – is primed and ready, Your Most Hygienic Highness," said Skweeky-Kleen. "It's all gleaming, dirt free and polished!"

"Oh yes, this is my favourite bit," said Commander Skrubbupp as he took his seat. "Now, what shall I set the dial to? So many great settings, so little time..."

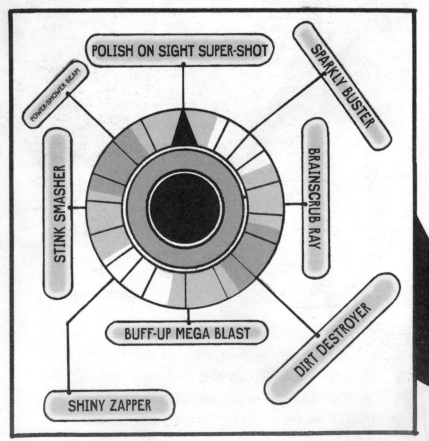

POLISH ON SIGHT SUPER-SHOT

SPARKLY BUSTER

POWER-SHOWER BEAM

STINK SMASHER

BRAINSCRUB RAY

BUFF-UP MEGA BLAST

DIRT DESTROYER

SHINY ZAPPER

"Hmmm," he pondered. **"The Brainscrub Ray!"**

"One blast and every parent on Earth will instantly become obsessed with cleanliness," said Skweeky-Kleen.

"These 'kids' won't know what's hit them!" said Skrubbupp.

"Loving your work, Oh Sorcerer of Shipshape," grovelled Skweeky-Kleen. "Loving your work!"

"Prepare to get tidy!" thundered Skrubbupp, pressing the **FIRE** button. The spaceship shuddered as a laser beam struck Earth...

"Now get me some soap," said Skrubbupp. "I'm sure this seat has traces of grubbiness..."

Earth was blasted by the Kleanon laser – a blue beam lighting up the night sky.

"What was *that*?" said Gerald.

Gerald, Gene and Fleabag were up late, trying to rebuild their rocket and make more Gross-Out Rocket Fuel. "Some sort of lightning?"

"It's not like any lightning I've ever seen before," said Gene. "It came from outer space."

"Very ug-strange," said Fleabag, who was more interested in the rocket fuel. "This stuff ug-stinks, but it wouldn't even ug-power an ug-ant into ug-space."

"Let's leave it for tonight," said Gene. "We'll get it to work tomorrow."

But when Gerald and Gene got to the Gross-Out Den the next morning, Gerald's parents were already there. And this time they didn't have a new item for the Museum – they had mops and buckets.

"What's going on?" whispered Gene. "I thought your parents were cool."

"They are," said Gerald. "This isn't like them at all. They've never asked Fleabag to clean his home before. Something's up!"

"Follow me," said Gene. "We need to sneak round the back to the alleyway!"

With Gerald's parents blocking the main door to the Den, Gerald and Gene used the secret back entrance instead.

"They've ug-been out there for ug-hours,"
said Fleabag, barricading the secret door again.

"We've got to stop them!" said Gerald, looking
through the keyhole. The parents were now pushing
up against the door, trying to get in.

"We need something to repel them!" said Gene,
desperately looking around the Den.

"Ug-Gross-Out ug-Rocket Fuel?" suggested Fleabag. He held up a test tube of stinking liquid.

"Great idea," said Gene. "Now all we have to do is dig a moat."

"We'll need a diversion," said Gerald. "There's only one thing for it... We'll have to sacrifice ourselves to save the Gross-Out Den!"

With that, he opened the door and soon had his parents' attention: "Hey, Dad, have you seen how messy *my* room is? And, Mum, you really must take Gene home to tidy *his* room!"

9 With Gerald's parents off the scene, Fleabag was able to dig a moat and fill it with the repulsive rocket fuel. The Gross-Out Den had been saved, but both Gerald and Gene had had to pay the price!

"I found enough dust on the shelves in my bedroom to stuff a pillow," complained Gerald as they headed to school.

"And I found seventeen pairs of old pants under my bed," said Gene.

"I just ug-hope the ug-rocket fuel keeps Gerald's parents ug-out of the Gross-Out Den," said Fleabag.

But at school they were in for an even bigger shock.

"Look how tidy everyone's bags are," whispered Gene. "Pencils in boxes, lunches in bubble wrap..."

"And what about the confiscation cupboard in the school hall?" hissed Gerald. Everything had been sorted, labelled and placed in alphabetical order.

"You'll be pleased to hear that I've cleaned up your film gear, even the film itself," said Mr Troutman proudly.

"All our footage destroyed?!" said Gerald. Another Gross-Out TV programme was gone for good!

"Now listen up, class," said Mr Troutman. "Today's lesson is why mops are good and mess is bad..."

"Something *is* going on," said Gerald. "But what?"

"I'm not sure, but I think that blue flash of light might have had something to do with it," replied Gene.

"The lesson is over," said Mr Troutman, handing every pupil a mop. "Let's all tidy the classroom!!!"

And the Kleanon attack was global. All around the world, parents were adopting a new hard-line on room-tidying.

Soon the whole planet would be unbearably shiny and clean...

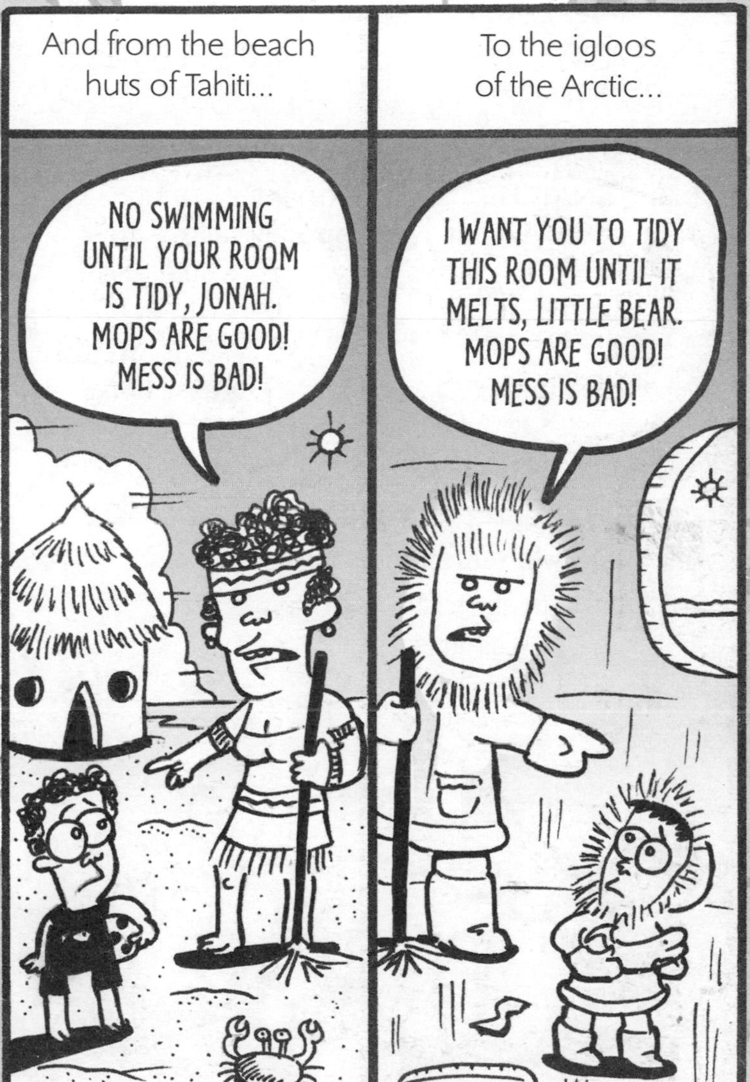

10 On the Kleanon ship, Commander Skrubbupp and his crew were gloating over a job well done.

"Shiny clean, shiny clean!" crowed Skrubbupp. "There will never be another untidy room on Earth, ever again! They have no idea how close they came to being **SNATCHED** and put on the Naughty Step with all the other really **GRUBBY** planets."

"Magnificent work, Oh Meticulously Muck-Free One!" said Skweeky-Kleen. "I have set a course back to Kleanon as you instructed."

"I think we should all take a well-earned rest," said Skrubbupp. "Let us return to our people and take pleasure in cleanliness with them once again."

But as Skweeky-Kleen fired up the engine, a small red light started to flash and a siren began to wail.

What's going on?"
said Skrubbupp. "Why
aren't we leaving?"

"The **Dirt-Detecting
Sensor** has picked
something up, sir,"
said Skweeky-Kleen.
"Something untidy on
Earth. I think it's an error
– it must be a software
issue. I'll call IT Support
when we get back.
Now, prepare for
blast off!"

But the red light was
flashing brighter and
the siren was getting
louder.

"We're not going
anywhere!" boomed
Skrubbupp. "There *is*
somewhere untidy
left on Earth! Get it
on screen now!!!"

"Yes, sir," said Skweeky-Kleen. "But I don't understand it – we zapped *all* the parents!"

As Skweeky-Kleen fiddled with the dials, a small building popped up on the screen.

"The 'Gross-Out Den'?!" roared Skrubbupp. "What is this place? Why is it still grubby?!"

"It seems to be completely resistant to parents," said Skweeky-Kleen. "*Something* is protecting it."

"This will never do. Prepare the **Travellator Pod**, and bring the mini-Kleansulator!" boomed Skrubbupp. "I'll just have to clean up this place myself! And it shall be tidied. **Oh yes, it shall be TIDIED!!!**"

Meanwhile, in the Gross-Out Den...

"All the parents may be obsessed by tidiness, but at least we can get away from them in here," said Gerald, as he nibbled on a sandwich.

"Too ug-right," said Fleabag. "Are you sure you don't want any ug-mouldy curry? The poppadoms are a lovely ug-green colour! "

"No, thanks," said Gene. He and Gerald were grateful to be able to hang out at Fleabag's, but they still didn't want to go anywhere near his food.

THROB

WOBBLE

Suddenly the Gross-Out Den began to shake and shudder.

"What's happening?" said Gerald.

"Something ug-seems to be ug-landing right outside!" said Fleabag excitedly.

"It's ... some sort of spaceship!" said Gerald. "**Aliens!** In our own backyard!!!"

"I'll ug-offer them some ug-rotten naan bread!" said Fleabag.

"I think we should stay right here," said Gene warily. "I don't think they're here to make friends."

Outside, two figures had emerged from a Travellator Pod.

"What kind of Children-People would live in a place like ... like *this*?" gasped Commander Skrubbupp. "And what *is* that stench?"

"My sensors are getting a mixture of prawn heads, squirrel droppings and toenail clippings." Skweeky-Kleen winced. "It seems to be a barrier to the hypnotized parents ... and us. We can't get any closer – the gases are making the Kleansulator malfunction!"

"**Barrier?!** These Children-People dare set up a barrier!" said Skrubbupp, holding his nose. "I know you can hear me in there!" he shouted.

"Don't move," warned Gene. "It's just as I feared. These aren't friendly aliens..."

"You dare defy *me*!" continued Skrubbupp. "I am Commander Skrubbupp, Leader of the Kleanons – the cleanest aliens in the galaxy. And I know you're in there. Well, thanks to your insolence, I declare Earth officially **GRUBBY**! And like all **GRUBBY** planets, it will be **SNATCHED** and put at the very back of the galaxy with all the other really **GRUBBY** planets!"

"Excellent, Oh Highly Polished One," said Skweeky-Kleen. "I will arrange for the **Vacuumiser** to be sent from Planet Kleanon at once. It will be here in a few days."

"Good. Let's see how they like having their planet sucked up by a huge spaceship and then spat out at the very back of the galaxy. Let's see how they enjoy having the Mucrons as next-door neighbours!" The commander cackled. "Now, get me away from this stinking hole and back to the mother ship! It's almost as bad as the Dust Mite Caverns of Surbitron 12."

And with that he pulled the cord on his Personal Shower Unit.

PING!

Skrubbupp and Skweeky-
Kleen reboarded the Travellator
Pod and blasted back to
Grub Buster 1.

Gerald, Gene and Fleabag
emerged on to the lawn. The
only trace of the aliens was a
large puddle of soapy water.

"Snatched by the
Vacuumiser?" said Gerald.
"The Mucrons? I don't like
the sound of this..."

"The Mucrons might be
ug-great, guys," said Fleabag.

"I don't think we should
risk finding out," said Gene.
"Time to get to work.
I've had an idea!"

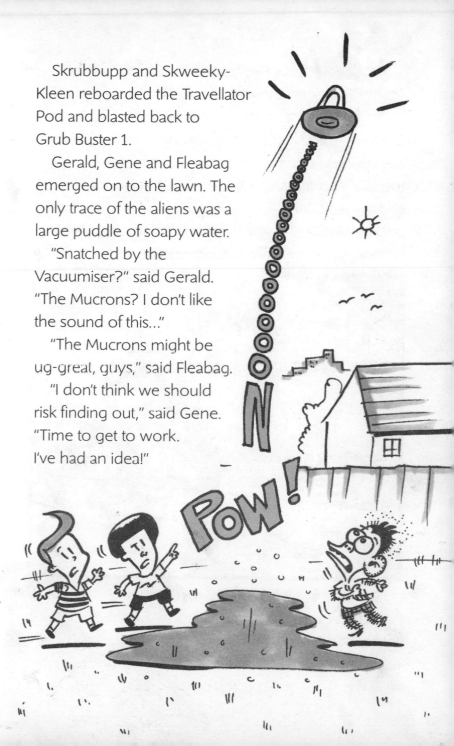

12 As we've already mentioned, Gene quite often has ideas, and as we've also mentioned, Gerald quite often thinks they're good ideas. The trouble is that Gene's ideas often land them in a heap of gross-out trouble. And this idea was ambitious, even by Gene's standards.

"To stop the Kleanons," said Gene, "we're going to have to sneak on to their spaceship."

"But how are we going to do that?" asked Gerald. "We can't even get our rocket to stay in the air!"

"That's down to the fuel," said Gene. "But we could do without fuel ... if we used **Gross-Out Power**. After all, this isn't a school project any more!"

"But we can't all ug-fit on the ug-Grossblaster," said Fleabag.

"We're not going to," said Gene. He held up a hastily drawn plan. "We're going to blast the Gross-Out Den into space!"

"Cool!" said Gerald. "Not even Chip Asteroid could compete with that – the first *outdoor* toilet in space! EVER!!!"

Gerald, Gene and Fleabag immediately set to work making the Gross-Out Den space worthy.

They battened down the windows and door with old bits of wood.

They installed reinforced glass in the roof.

They attached oxygen tanks to the walls.

And they even made space helmets out of old goldfish bowls.

The Gross-Out Den was finally ready for space!
"Cool! Let's go!" said Gerald.
"Ug-brilliant! I can't ug-wait," said Fleabag.

"There's one more thing," said Gene. "If we're going to get on-board the Kleanon ship, we're going to need ultra-tidy outfits... And I know just where to get them. Follow me."

13 First they went to Gene's Uncle Frederico, who owned a restaurant where the waiters were famous for their whiter than white shirts.

Then they went to Gerald's Auntie Mabel, who worked at a factory, making uniforms.

And finally they went to Mr Shiny Shoes, the local shoeshiner.

When they got back to the Gross-Out Den, Gerald's parents were there to meet them. Fortunately, when they saw the new clothes, they were delighted.

"Nice tidy clothes," said Gerald's mum.

"Tidy clothes are good! Untidy clothes are bad!" said Gerald's dad.

"Let's just hope these clothes fool the Kleanons," whispered Gene.

14 With the last-minute checks done, Gerald, Gene and Fleabag were ready.

"One last thing," said Gene, handing Fleabag a cup of stomach-turning liquid. "We're going to need to give you a boost!"

"Ug-delicious!" said Fleabag, before gulping down the bubbling fluid. "Ug-what was that?"

"Gross-Out Rocket Fuel!" said Gene. "We're going to need you to create the biggest turbo-fart ever..."

"It's the only way we're going to get the Gross-Out Den into space!" added Gerald.

With the rocket fuel bubbling in his belly, Fleabag took his position at the rear of the Den. And with a mighty heave, a horrible gurgling and a monstrous grumbling, finally there was...

The Gross-Out Den was roaring up, up and away!

"More power, Fleabag!" said Gene as they reached the Earth's atmosphere.

"You can do it!" said Gerald.

And with a final effort, Fleabag blasted them into space.

"You've done it!" said Gerald. "We're astronauts now!"

"I just hope we can get on-board the Kleanon ship without being noticed," said Gene. "We're on a direct course to meet it."

At the back of the ship, Fleabag tested out the theory of whether anyone can hear you burp in space...

16 But Gerald, Gene and Fleabag were being watched...

"Get me some eye drops. My eyeballs need cleaning." Skrubbupp winced as he observed the incoming craft on the screen. "What is *that*?"

"My sensors are picking up a construction of wood and glass, equipped with a primitive flushing mechanism," said Skweeky-Kleen. "It seems to be some sort of spacecraft made from an ... outdoor toilet!"

"We have seen many dirty things in space, but never a flying *toilet*." Skrubbupp shuddered. This planet really is too, too much. **Destroy that airborne lavatory at ONCE!**"

"But, my Overlord of Orderliness, the crew are all smartly dressed," said Skweeky-Kleen, watching the Gross-Out Den as it got closer. "Even the hairy one on the back is in a freshly ironed shirt."

"I recognize that building," said Skrubbupp. "It's that shack we visited on Earth!"

"These fine members of the community must be bringing it to us for destruction," said Skweeky-Kleen.

"Send out the Travellator Pod and welcome them aboard!" said Skrubbupp. "We'll invite them to join our crew. And do make sure the tow rope is cleaned – I'm sure our visitors will appreciate a *really* clean tow rope."

16

"**S**pacecraft incoming!" shouted Gerald. "We've been spotted!"

"Commander Skrubbupp would like to invite you on-board!" boomed the Kleanon pilot as the Pod drew alongside. "He wants you to join his crew!"

"This is great," said Gerald. "Our disguises are working!"

The Travellator Pod began towing the Gross-Out Den towards the Kleanon ship.

"When we're on-board, pretend to be neat and tidy," said Gene. "Then, when the moment is right, we'll use Fleabag's Gross-Out Power and take over the ship!"

As soon as they had docked, they were taken to meet Commander Skrubbupp.

"Welcome aboard," he said.

"We're just grateful to be away from grubby old Earth," said Gene. "Well, this place *is* neat and tidy."

"As a reward for bringing us the hut, I will tell you about our mission..." Skrubbupp said. "Earth is so grubby that we are going to suck it up with a giant vacuuming spaceship and banish it to the back of the galaxy. The Vacuumiser is currently being serviced on Kleanon, but it will be here soon."

"We've got to stop them!" whispered Gerald.

"Patience," said Gene. "We've done the hardest part – we're on-board."

"And as for that hovel, the Gross-Out Den – it will be destroyed at once," said Skrubbupp. **"Behold the Kleansulator!"**

"Surely that's not ug-necessary!" wailed Fleabag. "It may be an ug-toilet to you, but it's my ug-home!"

Skrubbupp and Skweeky-Kleen folded over with laughter.

"Living in a toilet?" Skrubbupp guffawed. "That's the best ever – not even a Mucron would do that!"

Gene quickly placed his hand over Fleabag's mouth. "You must excuse my friend," he said. "The high altitude seems to be affecting his brain." Then he whispered to Fleabag, "Sorry, Fleabag, but we need to make some sacrifices if we're going to save Earth."

"The high altitude does take some adjusting to," said Skrubbupp. "As a treat I will allow you – the neat hairy one – to operate the Kleansulator and smash that stinking pile of timber into a thousand pieces!"

"Go on," said Gerald, pushing a reluctant Fleabag forward. With a trembling upper lip, Fleabag raised a finger to press the "FIRE" button...

But suddenly Skweeky-Kleen interrupted. "We're getting some very interesting readings from that hut, sir," he said. "The grubbiness is off the scale. I think we should get our scientists to have a look at it."

"Very well," said Skrubbupp, before turning apologetically to Fleabag. "I'm so sorry ... and the FIRE button had been buffed specially."

"Maybe this will cheer you up..." he continued. "I have decided to record the **Grubby Snatching of Earth** for posterity purposes and I have invited two top journalists on to the ship. Skweeky-Kleen, show in the reporters from *Tidy!* magazine."

17 Skweeky-Kleen pressed a button and a door swooshed open. What was behind it shook Gerald, Gene and Fleabag to the sharp turn-ups of their well-pressed trousers.

In marched the Smugleys, dressed from top to toe in Kleanon uniforms! And it didn't take long for *Tidy!* magazine's newest reporters to rumble Gerald, Gene and Fleabag.

OH NO! IT'S THE SMUGLEYS!

"Horror! Horror!" wailed Mandy. "What are *they* doing here?"

"They were kind enough to deliver the Gross-Out Den," said Skrubbupp. "They are joining us to see Earth being snatched."

"But can't you see who they are?!" said Randy. "They are the untidiest, messiest, grossest people ever to have walked the Earth."

"They're our neighbours," said Mandy. "Gerald, Gene and Fleabag Monkeyface. It's *their* Den – it's where the hairy one LIVES!"

"Impostors?! On my ship?!" Skrubbupp trembled and released his Personal Shower Unit. "Skweeky-Kleen, set the Kleansulator to **Power-Shower Beam**. NOW!"

"There's been a misunderstanding!" cried Gene. "These reporters haven't researched their facts."

"Yes, we always dress like this," said Gerald. "We'd never seen the Gross-Out Den before today."

"I ug-love to be ug-tidy," insisted Fleabag.

But it was too late! The Power-Shower Beam blasted them with clean, soapy water, and their outfits were ruined!

Gerald, Gene and Fleabag were back to their usual selves, and Skrubbupp was not impressed.

"Euuuuk!" He winced, repeatedly tugging on his Personal Shower Unit. "Look at the Monkey-thing!"

"We can explain," said Gene. "You see we thought—"

"Enough!" barked Skrubbupp. "I know exactly what to do with you. You are going to become exhibits at Kleanon Zoo! And you'll be there in the blink of an eye, thanks to the **Transporter Ray**."

"Kleanon Zoo?" gulped Gerald.

"Yes – a zoo devoted to the messiest, grubbiest creatures in the universe," said Skweeky-Kleen.

"Quick, Fleabag," said Gene urgently. "Use some Gross-Out Power!"

But before Fleabag could so much as rustle up a turbo-sneeze or muster an earwax pellet, Skweeky-Kleen had programmed the Transporter Ray and pressed the button...

There was an eerie glow, followed by a loud bang! And the last thing Gerald, Gene and Fleabag saw before they were hurtled through space was the Smugleys – waving!

18 For what seemed like an eternity, but was actually only a few seconds, Gerald, Gene and Fleabag flew millions of light years through space.

"This is ug-fun," said Fleabag as his nostrils shuddered. "It ug-tickles!"

"So where is Planet Kleanon?" asked Gerald as his head shook.

"I'm not sure, but it feels like a long way," said Gene as his face wobbled.

With a thud, the three space travellers landed on a sparkling clean floor. A Kleanon with a clipboard was there to meet them...

KLEANON ZOO

THUD!

"Welcome to your new home," he said. "I'm Warden Spikkenspan, Head of Kleanon Zoo, and you must be the Children-People. I've been expecting you. You're even more gross than I was told. The public are going to love you! Now let me show you to your pen."

With no obvious means of escape, Gerald, Gene and Fleabag meekly followed the warden.

As they walked through the zoo, the warden proudly pointed out the other exhibits...

Here we have the unkempt **Booffon Crabs of Follicle 19**. They never comb their hair – not once, during their entire lives!

In there are the many-pimpled **Spottleflott Donkeys of the Chattersplax Galaxy**. They have the worst skin in the universe!

"And here are your living quarters," said Spikkenspan, opening the door to a cramped room. "You will be fed rotten bananaflax three times a day. Visiting is from 29 o'clock. Oh and you'll be pleased to hear that the Vacuumiser is almost ready to leave for Earth. **What a shame your home planet is going to be SNATCHED!**"

With that, he slammed the door and turned the key. Gerald, Gene and Fleabag were left to begin life in their new home: Kleanon Zoo.

19

"This place isn't so ug-bad," said Fleabag the next morning as he tucked into rotten bananaflax. "I can't ug-wait to meet the other ug-guys."

"Sorry, Fleabag, *you* may have found paradise, but we've got to save Earth from being vacuumed away to a far corner of the galaxy," said Gene.

"This place looks Gross-Out-Power proof," said Gerald, as he examined the walls.

"We'll need to find another way out," said Gene. "We're going to need an idea ... and soon!"

While Gene desperately tried to come up with a plan, they all got to know their fellow inmates. They soon discovered they had lots in common!

"There are lovers of gross-out in every corner of the galaxy," said Gerald as he played cards with a Spottleflott Donkey.

"Yes, there really is gross-out everywhere," said Gene as he arm-wrestled a giant Amoeba. "And Fleabag has grown very fond of Baby Mucron!"

"He's even ug-grosser than I ug-am," said Fleabag as they wallowed in space mud.

But every day, at 29 o'clock, the atmosphere changed. All the aliens were herded from their cages to greet the visitors – and they were horrible!

Kleanon kids may have been tidy, but that didn't stop them from being the most badly behaved children in the universe. Each one came equipped with household cleaners, bars of soap and disinfectants, which they squirted and threw at the exhibits.

"OK, even I'm ug-ready to leave now," said Fleabag, shaking disinfectant out of his hair.

 Finally, Gene had an idea.

"It's so obvious – I should have thought of it right away!" he said. "What do we have in common with everyone here?"

"We all love all things gross?" suggested Gerald.

"Yes, but as well as that?" said Gene.

"We all love ug-rotten bananaflax," said Fleabag. "Apart from ug-you two ... oh and the ug-Mucron, who prefers rancid ug-broccolox."

"YES!" said Gene. "But *as well as all that*: we all want to escape."

"Of course," said Gerald.

"Individually we may not be able to break out of here, but if we all join forces, maybe *we* can..."

At feeding time, Gene explained his plan to the aliens. And it didn't take long to get them all on-board.

"If everyone does their job we can't fail," said Gene.

"Let's hope so," said Gerald.

That night the exhibits of Kleanon Zoo put Gene's most daring plan ever into action...

First of all the Mmmm-Z Plants got the guards' attention by throwing mud at the window...

Then the Spottleflott Donkeys slimed them...

WHAT'S GOING ON IN THERE?

GET THESE SPOTTY BRUTES AWAY FROM ME!

The giant Amoebas herded them into a corner...
AWAY, YOU HIDEOUS BEASTS!
Then Baby Mucron covered them in toxic mucous...
THE MUCRON IS REVOLTING!
And finally, the Booffon Crabs dropped them into a filthy tank...
THIS IS UNBEARABLE!
Where their Flotation Pods fizzed, spluttered and then fell apart.
GET US OUT AT ONCE!

"Just as I'd hoped," said Gene triumphantly. "Their high-tech equipment couldn't withstand an onslaught of gross-out!"

"They should be stuck there long enough for us to make a getaway," said Gerald.

But, suddenly, out of nowhere, Warden Spikkenspan appeared. "What's going on here?" he shouted. "Nobody move or I'll use the zoo's Kleansulator. You're familiar with the **Power-Shower Beam**, I believe?!"

But Fleabag wasn't about to face another soapy soaking.

"Ug-never again!" he said, and bionic-belched Spikkenspan into the aquarium. Everyone cheered!

"Now let's ug-get out of here!" Fleabag said.

KA-HAAA!

SPLOOSH!

Outside the zoo, Gerald, Gene and Fleabag got their first taste of Planet Kleanon.

"I've never seen such a glittery spotless place." Gene shuddered as he looked around at the highly polished buildings and sparkling clean roads.

But there was no time to spare – they had to escape, and fast! The aliens quickly jumped into the guards' Travellator Pods.

"We'll be home in no time in these," said one of the Booffon Crabs.

Gerald, Gene and Fleabag waved goodbye to the zoo creatures, until they were all gone.

"Now we've got to get to the Vacuumiser before it sets off for Earth," said Gene.

"These might help," said Gerald.

"Kleanon uniforms!"

21 Meanwhile, on Grub Buster 1, Commander Skrubbupp and Skweeky-Kleen were waiting impatiently.

"What's the delay?" fussed Skrubbupp. "How long does it take to prepare a Vacuumiser?"

"They are fitting a new bag, Oh Spring-Cleaned Astounding One," said Skweeky-Kleen. Just then a screen caught his eye. "Look, a newsflash on **Kleanon TV**."

22 Dressed as Kleanons, our three intrepid space travellers embarked on the cleanest, but most dangerous journey of their lives – in search of the Vacuumiser.

"Whatever you do, don't turn the shower on!" warned Gene. "It's bad enough having to wear these shiny clean uniforms, but a warm shower... Yuck!"

They were getting lots of strange looks, but their costumes seemed to be working.

103

And being in disguise gave them the chance to have a good look around. And everywhere was shockingly spotless!

"It certainly looks clean, but it doesn't smell so fresh," said Gerald, holding his nose.

"What *is* that stench?" said Gene. "Fleabag?"

But for once the disgusting smell wasn't coming from Fleabag – it was coming from Baby Mucron. He was tucked inside Fleabag's Kleanon uniform!

"Baby Mucron?!" said Gerald. "What's *he* doing here?"

"He doesn't have an ug-home to go to," said Fleabag sadly. "His ug-mum's at the other ug-end of the ug-galaxy on the ug-**Intergalactic Naughty Step**. Can he ug-come with us?"

"I will help you save Earth," said Baby Mucron in a very cute, tiny voice. "I know where the Vacuumiser is hidden. I heard the wardens talking about it."

23

With the Mucron giving directions, they soon arrived at a huge Space Station on the edge of town. Looming over the neat and tidy area was a vast spacecraft... **The Vacuumiser!** "Now all we have to do is get on-board," said Gerald, as he observed the sinister spaceship.

"Well, the Kleanons hate anything dirty," said Gene, "so we just need to find the grossest part of the spaceship, and hide there."

"The **Space Toilet**!" said Gerald. "There must be a sewage pipe that leads to it. Maybe we can use it to sneak on-board?"

"Ug-great idea!" said Fleabag approvingly.

"It's worth a try," said Gene.

"Of course, this Kleanon craft is a lot less advanced than our Mucron spaceship," mocked Baby Mucron as they searched for the pipe.

"Just as I'd hoped," said Gerald, pointing to a large, shiny clean pipe. "All we have to do is climb up and we're on-board!"

Suddenly they heard a voice – they had been spotted by a Kleanon guard!

"Who are you?" he barked. "This area is off limits!"

"Er ... we're here to ... er ... clean up," stuttered Gene.

"Yes, we've been told that Commander Skrubbupp wants the ship to be even cleaner than usual," added Gerald.

"No one told *me* about any extra cleaning," said the guard. "In fact, I've been told to keep a lookout for fugitives from the zoo. Did you know Baby Mucron is on the loose? It makes you grateful to have a Personal Shower Unit!"

With that, the guard turned his shower on and looked expectantly at Gerald, Gene and Fleabag.

"Yes, of course." Gerald winced before adding, as enthusiastically as he could, "Let's *all* use our personal showers!"

The three of them closed their eyes, cringing as the soapy water covered them. But the guard was satisfied, and he left them to get on with their "work".

24 Gerald, Gene, Fleabag and Baby Mucron
began to crawl up the pipe to the Space Toilet,
and for once they were grateful for the Kleanons'
love of all things clean – the pipe was spotless!

"The **Space Toilet**!" said Gene, climbing out.
"The perfect place to hide."

"First let's get these horrible clean uniforms off!"
said Gerald.

Suddenly the spaceship began to rumble and roar
– they'd made it on-board just in time!

"We'll wait until we're well away from Planet Kleanon
before we take control of the ship," said Gene.

"Just ug-kick back and ug-enjoy the ride," said Fleabag,
who was loving space travel on a
Space Toilet.

"Anytime now," said the Mucron, looking out of the window. "We just passed Marzipax 11."

They quietly approached the main deck of the Vacuumiser and peered inside.

"How do we overpower them?" pondered Gene.

"Leave it to me," squeaked Baby Mucron, stepping forward. "To the Kleanons, I am the most feared alien in the cosmos. Not only can I blow myself up to twice my normal size, but I can also fire toxic slimeballs *and* I have the worst breath in the universe!"

"Now those are some ug-Gross-Out Powers *I'd* like to ug-have!" said Fleabag, impressed by his new little friend's skills.

Gerald, Gene and Fleabag hid in the doorway and watched...

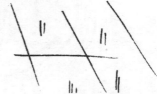

Silently, the Mucron snuck up on the Kleanon crew.
"Boo!" he said.

"A Mucron stowaway!" screeched the pilot.

"Dirty Mucron! Go away!" screamed a crewman.

As soon as Baby Mucron started to inflate, mass panic set in...

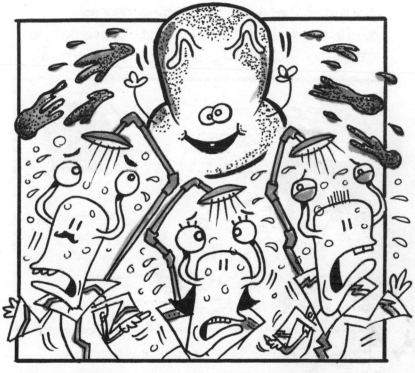

The Kleanons fled, shrieking and operating their personal showers. They ran to the Travellator Pod as fast as they could.

With the Kleanon crew blasting their way home, the task now was to stop the Vacuumiser from reaching Earth.

"It seems to be on autopilot," said Gene, looking at the vast control panel. "I've got no idea how to override it, never mind fly this thing."

Not even the Mucron knew how to fly the Vacuumiser, and they were running out of time, fast! Then Gene noticed a large red button.

"The Transporter Ray!" he said. "If *we* can't fly the ship, then maybe we can beam in someone who can!"

"Chip Asteroid!" said Gerald. "He can fly anything!"

"I hope I can get it to work," said Gene, tapping at the computer. "You type the name here ... and the destination here ... then you press this button here..."

There was a loud bang and standing before them was astronaut and intergalactic TV hunk Chip Asteroid!

"*You* again!" said Chip. "Where am I? And what is that *thing*?"

"You've been teleported to the deck of a Vacuumiser spaceship and that *thing* is Baby Mucron," said Gerald. "He's actually very friendly."

"Aha! That makes me the first man EVER to be transported to a Vacuumiser spaceship," said Chip proudly. "Not to mention the first—"

"This ship is set to suck up Earth and stick it at the back of the galaxy," interrupted Gene. "We need your extraordinary knowledge of spaceships to override the autopilot and fly this thing."

"Override ... autopilot? Fly a *real* ... spaceship..." stuttered Chip. "I'd love to, but ... er ... sorry, I can't help."

"But Earth is depending on you," said Gene.

"That's all very well, but no can do," said Chip. "Now if you could kindly send me home, I've got a cake in the oven. You see my mummy is popping over and ... well, this looks really complicated."

"What about all your journeys to the space station and beyond?" said Gene. "Flipping pancakes? Plumping pillows? You know everything there is to know about space flight."

"We've all seen you do it on TV," added Gerald.

"Yes, it's all very impressive," said Chip. "But..."

"But ug-what?" said Fleabag impatiently.

"Filmed in a studio," said Chip in a quiet voice. "All of it. I have the best special-effects team in the business..."

"So you've never actually flown a spacecraft before – EVER?" said Gerald.

"I've watched the stuntmen do it." Chip sighed. "But this is real – it's far too scary for me."

"But think of the headlines if you pull it off!" said Gene.

"I suffer from chronic space-travel sickness," said Chip, looking at the daunting array of buttons and dials.

"You'd be a real hero," said Gene. "Not a fake one – you might even get a medal!"

"A medal? Now that *would* nice!" said Chip, warming to the challenge. "Right, you're on. This is it! This is real! **Let's fly this baby!!!**"

26 Far across the galaxy, Commander Skrubbupp was watching their every move on a large screen.

"So that explains why we lost communication with the Vacuumiser," he fumed, spitting out his cheesy bread. "Clean these crumbs up at once!"

"Of course, Oh Sultan of Spotless," said Skweeky-Kleen, spraying and polishing the screen. "We should have known this would happen as soon as we heard about the mass breakout at Kleanon Zoo."

"And they think they can just take control of the ship and all their problems will go away." Skrubbupp chuckled. "Wait until they find out what we've got in store for them!"

"We're not scared of Baby Mucron! Pathetic!" Skweeky-Kleen guffawed.

"Oh, this is good," said Randy, who'd been taking notes throughout. "This is *too* good. It's the perfect ending to our article for *Tidy!* magazine."

"This will make the cover for sure!" said Mandy. "I can almost smell the Press Award!"

Unaware of the Kleanon threat, Chip Asteroid had finally managed to get the Vacuumiser under control.

"I can do this!" he cried. "I'm a real hero! I'm the first man EVER to fly a Kleanon ship! I want my medal right now!"

"The job's not over yet," said Gene. "Skrubbupp is still out there. We've got to stop him for good!"

"Why don't we give him a dose of his own medicine," said Gerald. "Let's suck *him* up!"

"Great idea!" said Gene. "Set a course for Grub Buster 1."

"Let's do it!" said Chip, using the homing device to set a course for Skrubbupp's ship.

"This is easy," said Chip, as they sped across the galaxy.

"Too easy," said Gene, as the Kleanon ship came into view. "Surely they've spotted us."

"This should do it," said Gerald, pressing a button.

The huge vacuumising nozzle at the front of the ship started to creak into position.

"It's ug-pointing straight at ug-Skrubbupp's ship!" said Fleabag. "Let 'em ug-have it!"

"This is going to be *gooooood*!" said Baby Mucron.

"Take aim," said Gene, "and FIRE!"

"It's suction time!" said Gerald.

But nothing happened...

"What's going on?" said Gene, peering outside.

"The suction nozzle has been disabled," said Gerald.

Suddenly Commander Skrubbupp appeared on a giant screen...

28 With a jerk, the Vacuumiser was pulled at a terrifying speed through space – and no matter how hard Chip tried to regain control of the ship, the engine of Grub Buster 1 was just too powerful.

"It's getting darker and darker out there," said Gene.

"At least it's just us and not Earth being snatched," said Gerald bravely.

Finally, they started to slow down...

"This is it," said Baby Mucron. "This is the very back of the universe."

On a giant step were perched all the gross planets that the Kleanons had snatched...

Quorklork 3
Home to the disgustingly dirty Worm-men

Zefron ZZZ
Land of the garbage-eating Filthweasles

Plantifrax 11
Here the cave-dwelling Slugoids feast on dead insects

Mucroid
Home planet of the grossest creatures in the universe – the Mucrons!

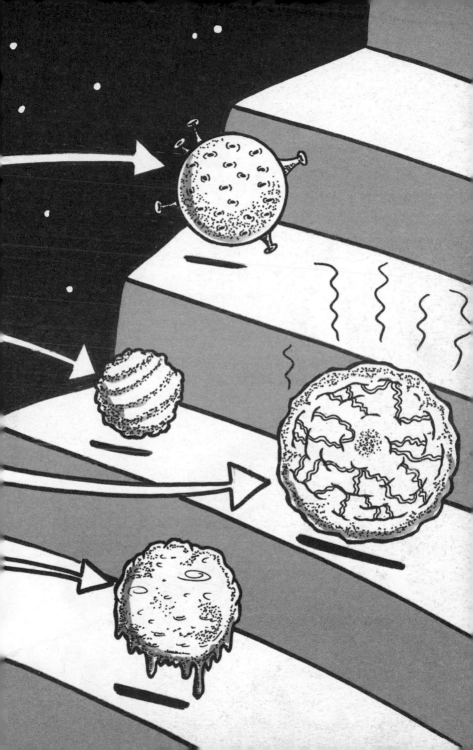

Grub Buster 1 finally stopped.

"We're being lowered into position," said Gene. "Right next to Planet Mucroid."

Skrubbupp's face once again appeared on the screen. "Welcome to your new home," he said. "Your ship has been disabled so you will stay here for ever! And don't worry – we've sent for a new Vacuumiser ship. You will be joined by your filthy home planet very soon!"

"I knew I should never have gone into space!" wailed Chip. "Please spare me! We give up! Take us home!"

"We've got to stop them – and fast!" said Gene. "But how are we going to get out of this ship?"

"Mummy will help us!" said Baby Mucron. "She can *blast* us on to their ship."

"Of course," said Gene. "The Transporter Ray! We can bring Queen Mucron to *us*!"

"Ug-quickly!" said Fleabag urgently.

Gene pressed a button and BANG! – there before them was a fully grown Mucron!

Queen Mucron was delighted to see her baby again and she couldn't wait to get her dirty green mitts on Skrubbupp and his crew.

"Jump on my back," she said. "This should be fun!"

With everyone holding on, Queen Mucron used a toxic slimeball to blast out into space.

"We've got to climb the tow rope before they release it!" said Gene.

"Free the tow rope!" squealed Skrubbupp as the huge green creature began climbing towards them.

"The tow rope is stuck!!!" wailed Skweeky-Kleen.

Queen Mucron crashed through the window and into the Kleanon ship!

"Eeek!" cried Skweeky-Kleen. "There's untidiness everywhere!"

"The game's up Skrubbupp – your days of cleaning up the universe are over," said Gene.

"That's where you're wrong!" cried out Skrubbupp, dodging Queen Mucron's breath. "You see, all we have to do is step through this escape hatch and blast our way home using our shower units as jetpacks!"

"And don't think you can catch us. The Travellator Pod is long gone, along with the rest of the crew ... and the ship is out of fuel!" crowed Skweeky-Kleen.

"Enjoy your new home!"

"Are you sure this hatch was cleaned?" asked Skrubbupp as they jumped to freedom.

"I'll never be able to keep up," said Queen Mucron.

"There is one craft left that could work," said Gene. **The Gross-Out Den!"**

"Ug-home sweet ug-home!" said Fleabag, who couldn't wait to be reunited with his beloved toilet.

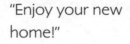

29 Fortunately, the Kleanons hadn't got round to destroying the Den and it was still tethered to the back of the ship.

Leaving Chip to guard Grub Buster 1, Gerald, Gene and the two Mucrons quickly leapt inside, while Fleabag (who had kept an emergency flask of Gross-Out Rocket Fuel up his sleeve) turbo-farted them through space in pursuit of Skrubbupp and Sweeky-Kleen.

"Hold on ug-tight," he said.

"This is way cool!" said Baby Mucron. "You've got to show me how you do that!"

Skrubbupp and Skweeky-Kleen twisted and turned, but they couldn't shake off the Gross-Out Den. And they were finally cornered just outside Plantifrax 11.

"This is unbearable!" howled Skrubbupp.
"My Personal Shower Unit needs refilling!"

"Now the game really is up," said Gene. "Unless
you promise to leave the galaxy alone for ever you'll
have to stay here and become Slugoid food!"

"Our mission is over, we promise," wheedled
Skrubbupp. "All we want to do is go back to Kleanon
and stay there."

"Good choice. Queen Mucron is going to fly you
home – just as soon as you've freed all the planets
on the Naughty Step," said Gerald. "Enjoy the ride!"

It was time to say a fond farewell to the Mucrons. But first Fleabag explained the art of turbo-farting to Baby Mucron. On the way home, Gerald, Gene and Fleabag stopped at Grub Buster 1 to pick up Chip and put the ship out of action for good. With the auto-destruct set, they were about to leave when Chip heard a small squeaky voice. Hiding at the back of the spacecraft were the Smugleys.

"Can we come with you, please?" wheedled Mandy Smugley. "We've had enough space travel for now."

"We promise to be good," begged Randy.

"I suppose so," said Gene. "There are first-class seats for you, right next to Fleabag!"

"In an ug-prime position to see me ug-turbo-fart all the way ug-home!" Fleabag chuckled.

The Smugleys did their best to block their noses, but they had to endure the worst trip of their lives as Fleabag's Gross-Out Power blasted them all back to Earth.

30 When Gerald, Gene and Fleabag put the Gross-Out Den back in its usual place (after dropping Chip off at his TV studio), Gerald's parents were there to meet them.

"Look, we found an ancient pork chop behind the fridge," said Gerald's mum.

"We thought you could use it for your rocket fuel," said Gerald's dad.

"Looks like things have got back to normal," whispered Gerald.

"And there's someone here to meet the Smugleys too!" Gene chuckled, spotting Claudio Click.

"I think I'll just ug-put this pork chop in the Museum for ug-now," said Fleabag when they were back in the Den. "We need an ug-break from ug-space travel. Now who's for ug-tea? I could give it a kick with the last of the rocket fuel?"

But Gerald and Gene had had enough of *all* things space age.

"I've got a better idea," said Gerald. "Why don't we see if Claudio Click and the Smugleys are thirsty?"

"Unreal!" said Gene. "And we can use the brand-new film gear that Chip gave us to record it!"

To find out more, read the next "Disgusting Adventure of Fleabag Monkeyface", which makes this one seem like a spring-clean on Planet Kleanon. **Don't say we didn't warn you!!!**

If you can't wait until the next
Fleabag Monkeyface book, here's
a free comic to keep you going.
(It makes perfect on-the-toilet reading!)

A DISGUSTING MINI ADVENTURE

FLEABAG COMIX

ISSUE #4 FREE!

IT'S NO CRIME TO SLIME!

YOUR PASSPORT TO PONGINESS!

Baby Mucron's Guide to REALLY REALLY GROSS PLANETS

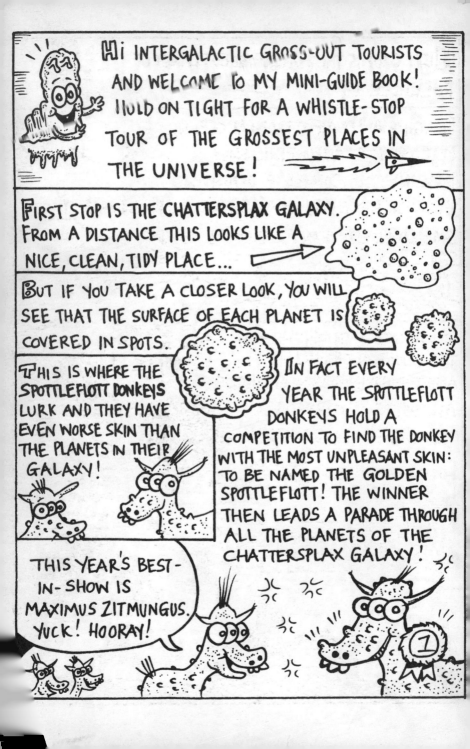

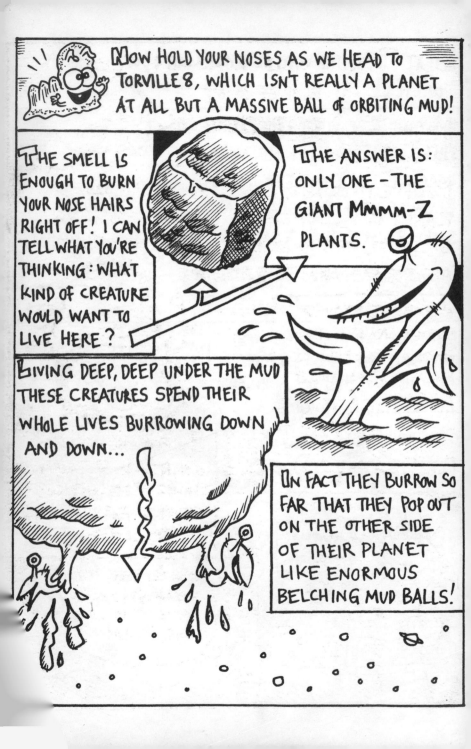